"There." Derek pointed.

A woman huddled under a pedestrian overpass, slight, with messy brown hair. Sarah's first instinct: If we cleaned her up, with those cheekbones, she'd be a perfect Serenity Curator. She huddled with a blanket over her shoulders—Las Vegas nights get cold—holding a sign that said "Homeless, anything helps." Sarah looked from Derek and back to herself. They both had the appearance of harmless suburbanites, nothing about either one of them suggested murderers.

"Go get her," Sarah said.

"We both know it'll be easier if you do it."

He was right, but she didn't want to admit it, and played dumb. "Why's that?"

Derek gave her a look. "She'll trust you. Come on, if some dude approaches you, you'd freak out. But if a woman came up to you...?"

DOWNLINES

KRISTIN DEARBORN

Introduction

Monsters can wear many guises. Some monsters are terrifying when they reveal their true selves: lizard people, vampires, and werewolves. Kristin Dearborn's "Downlines" explores a faceless, intangible monstrosity that can be far more dangerous to body and soul: A system.

The entity at the center of "Downlines" is a creature that has sunk its claws into millions of Americans and left many of them ruined: the multi-level marketing organization. MLMs dangle the hope that they'll make you rich, all with a little bit of elbow-grease and pep, while often preying on women (especially stay-at-home-moms) who are eager to make some extra money to supplement their incomes.

But what do those new MLM representatives have to give up to reach the kind of success their recruiting reps promote on social media? What's hiding behind those carefully crafted images of big houses, happy kids and adoring spouses?

I adore Kristin's horror for its deft combination of monsters with a social critique, and she has the perfect eye for capturing the dark side of modern capitalism.

Life in the world's richest nation certainly still holds plenty of advantages, but growing inequality amid a rich-get-richer economy means that some people will resort to *anything* to achieve the American dream. And is it a downline's fault that they have fallen prey to MLMs that promises them an easy foothold into a better life?

Well, you'll have to judge for yourself, but it's clear that killing a lizard person or vampire might just be a lot easier than slaying one of capitalism's Big Bads.

—Aimee Picchi, Nebula finalist for short fiction

Downlines

In the media room of the police station, harsh camera lights illuminated each and every imperfection on Derek Freidman's handsome face. "I just want my wife and my daughters back. Please. If you're out there, honey, or if anyone knows…" His voice broke, and he shielded his eyes, rimmed red from crying, from the brightness. Standing alone on a media dais, he fidgeted. He twitched. He scanned the cops and reporters, begging permission from one of them to relinquish the spotlight. He was a builder, not a public speaker.

Sarah flattened herself against the wall, making herself as small and unnoticeable as she could. No way was she getting up there. Her stomach churned—nausea from not having eaten, from dreading all the attention raining down on Derek. Nausea because her best friend was missing. It wasn't right. None of it was right.

Cassiopeia hadn't called after her doctor's appointment, which wasn't like her. She'd usually call Sarah from the car, cursing at traffic and babbling out a stream of consciousness about her day, about Derek, about everything. Cassie's

Facebook lay dormant, none of the daily videos she usually posted, not even a meme. No texts. That had been noon yesterday, now it was almost six, Sarah hadn't eaten since breakfast, when the police finally decided to do something about the missing person, and her stomach howled.

If *only* Cassie were missing, that would be one thing. Officer Maxwell told them he couldn't file a missing person report on an adult unless they'd been missing for seventy-two hours. It wasn't just Cassie missing, though. Miri and Arwen were missing too, and even if they were with their Mommy, the fact that one parent couldn't find them escalated the whole matter to code red. Sarah wondered if the police used actual color coding for emergencies. She wasn't sure.

Thing was, the husband always did it. Everyone knew that. She watched him, the way his eyes darted, his knee jumped. He wasn't like that. He was a chill guy. He'd changed ever since Serenity came into their lives. Since Cassie got successful. Sarah's phone buzzed, and she glanced at it.

ANY WORD? From Petra, one of Cassie's downlines.

NOTHING YET.

They'd have to put out a statement of some kind soon, she knew. Cassie's fans and customers were already getting antsy. Sarah silenced her own Facebook notifications because the whole thing was blowing up.

Derek stepped to the side, next to Sarah, and she involuntarily took a step back. An imposing police officer took the microphones, sharing what they knew.

Derek left for work at 5:30 that morning, kissing his sleeping wife goodbye.

The girls didn't show up for daycare at eight. When the provider tried to call Cassie, it went straight to voicemail.

Yesterday, Cassie missed her 10:00 AM ultrasound. Cassie was twenty-one weeks pregnant. Sarah hadn't known that detail, exactly how far along, but Cassie promised to find out if the baby was a boy or a girl and tell her. Derek said he didn't want to know. Probably because he didn't want another girl. When Cassie hadn't answered calls or texts or Facebook Messenger or Instagram or Signal or even the Serenity app, Sarah assumed another miscarriage and hurried to the house. Cassie's car was there, the doors were locked, and the house carried an unsettling empty feeling.

She'd called Derek, gotten his voicemail, then called the cops. They didn't much care, but then, after twenty-four hours, they'd decided they *were* concerned about the missing children.

The house. They'd purchased it a year ago—a year ago next week, after Cassie's first big break with Serenity. Her first five-figure bonus. Sarah remembered her happy tears. *I'm good at this. I'm finally actually good at something!* She'd lost fifty pounds on the Serenity plan. Six months ago she'd pushed Derek into it, and he'd lost forty. They both looked so good. Now Cassie so cute with her baby bump. And the girls, three and four, were precious. They made a perfect family.

But Cassie was missing and the husband always did it. Sarah hated to jump to conclusions, but she couldn't think of any other way her beautiful, vibrant friend would just disappear.

"You have a shake packet on you?" Derek whispered in her ear. His breath was hot and wet, and blew her mermaid-colored hair back.

"I had my last one for lunch," Sarah lied. Marissa would be so unimpressed. They were expected to have product on them at all times; it wasn't the Serenity way to tell a paying customer "no." Sarah thought she had some of the shakes at home…or maybe she'd sold them all? Unlike Cassie, Sarah wasn't particularly good at this. Just good enough, she liked to think.

Derek deflated. "My app is going off. They say I can't go back to the house. I don't want to go back. I just…" He sighed, and the sigh terminated in a sob, hitching in his throat. She didn't want to comfort him. A handful of local reporters congregated like a school of fish.

The police took the situation seriously because of the children involved. Right now, officers canvassed the Freidmans' neighborhood, going door to door with fliers showing Cassie's, Arwen's, and Miri's smiling faces. Updated photos were never an issue, Cassie lived with her phone in her hand. It was important for her customers to see her as a real person, to experience life with her step by step. As Marissa liked to remind Sarah, she could have taken a page or two out of Cassie's book. "Talk to them. Let them see the real you. They won't want to work with you unless they understand you. Walk them through how to use the app."

This morning, when the officer had pointed at an iPhone in a pink designer case and asked, "Is this her phone?" Sarah's guts clenched. It would have been less jarring to see Cassie's manicured hand severed on the kitchen counter. That phone was her lifeline. When Derek tapped the screen, the red low-battery icon flashed weakly at him.

Sarah knew the phone would blow up as soon as they plugged it in. Did Derek know the password? Sarah did, but she wasn't sure if Cassie wanted Derek to see what was on it.

"I've got a charger in my purse," she said.

"There's one here," Derek took the phone across the kitchen to a charging station by the fridge. The number of chargers Cassie kept spoke to her devotion to the device. They littered the house and car. She was never more than ten feet from one.

———————

A memory drifted to Sarah—she and Cassie at last year's Serenity conference, floating in the pool, drinks in hand, well past curfew. The hotel switched the main lights off, and the submerged ones in the pool turned everything blue. The glows of their phones lit their faces.

"If I left my phone behind, I could go anywhere."

Sarah hadn't really been listening. Kaitlynne posted about crossing the $10K net month threshold, and Sarah was trying to find the perfect emojis to celebrate. She was pretty drunk, seeing double, and kept hitting the wrong emoji, the one next to the red balloon was two creepy people… Geishas? They were next to a Chinese lantern, so they were something Asian. She didn't want to accidentally share that on Kaitlynne's post, everyone would think she was such a weirdo.

"Kaitlynne had —"

"Leave the phone behind, leave my wallet, take the girls, and vanish. I'd have to prep for it, need money stored up. I couldn't use a credit card or an ATM card. Leaving all that behind, they'd assume I was dead."

Sarah's drunk brain spun like a tire not getting traction. "Why would you do that?" She'd just need to download the Serenity app on a new phone if she did that. "And you can't disappear if you're drinking Serenity."

Cassie waved her away with an overexaggerated, slightly drunk sweep of her hand. "Don't you ever get bored?"

"Um, no. I have everything I want. What about Derek?" It was true, Sarah realized. She did have everything. Her cute little condo, enough money to get her hair and nails done without feeling guilty. It was petty, but that'd been the barometer to let her know she'd made it.

"Derek hasn't loved me for a long time."

Sarah gawked at her. "What are you talking about? He'd do anything for you. He's so good about watching the girls and helping around the house. He totally loves you."

"He's trapped, I'm trapped. We're all trapped. I could even leave the girls with him when I go."

"Don't you want another baby?"

She was quiet. Last year she'd had a miscarriage. So brave, she told all of her Serenity followers about it on Facebook Live, tears streaming down her face.

Derek ripped a door off the hinges he was so mad. She hadn't told him first. His friend Chris heard from his girlfriend Peggy who'd seen Cassie's Facebook Live. He put his fist through the drywall, leaving a bloody smudge Sarah saw the next day. By nightfall, it was plastered and painted, just a little bit cleaner than the rest of the wall.

"It's the only thing that keeps him interested," she said sullenly. "He likes the kids more than he likes me."

Sarah chewed on that. Wasn't it supposed to be so? Your kids were everything, the whole world. It was why she didn't want them. If she were to get married, and she wasn't sure she wanted that, she wanted her man to love her most of all.

"I could be someone new. Do something new. Make up the whole story for myself."

Sarah knew Cassie married her first husband young, came from a very poor section of West Virginia, somehow sprouted wings and now lived here in the outskirts of Las Vegas. "The desert is better for my skin," she liked to say.

Sarah wondered if somewhere in West Virginia there was a family searching for a missing woman who looked a lot like Cassie.

———————

The press conference ended and Sarah took a deep breath, then approached Officer Maxwell, who'd been the first to respond to the call, and also had been with them all day.

"Can I talk to you?" She hated how small her voice sounded. Meek and scared.

"Of course."

"In private?"

Officer Maxwell cut a glance at Derek, and they stepped out of the police station into the sweltering night. To the south, Las Vegas lit the sky orange. She told Maxwell about the pool conversation. She left out the part about the Serenity app. One didn't talk about Serenity to people on the outside, not even the cops. Maxwell chewed on his lip as he listened, ending with, "Interesting." He stared off at the horizon, the glow of the city. "Why don't you head home, Ms. Perrin. We'll let you know if we find anything."

Sarah wanted to argue, wanted to say they couldn't just dismiss her, but they could. She wasn't family. She was just a friend. In all likelihood, the husband had done it. She kept herself together until she slid behind the wheel of her Camry, and then she cried.

She looked at her phone. Pulled up Cassie's Insta. Her last picture was from this year's conference just a day ago. A video taken with a backdrop of pools and palms, talking about how much fun she'd had but how she'd almost left a day early to get back to her family because she missed them. "I didn't, though," Cassie beamed at her camera. "I know how important me-time is, and I need all you ladies who are struggling to remember that, too."

The first wave of messages had been sympathetic, the second vitriolic. "How could you just leave him?" "Maybe you should live your life in the present and not just be on social all the damned time." "Derek is single? Sign me up!!" How nasty and shallow could people be.

A text from a strange number.

MEET ME AT THE HOUSE.

Crying, it froze her in her tracks, stopped her breathing. A...wrong number? She knew who it was before the next message:

THIS IS DEREK. NEW PHONE.

Why would he get a new phone if he wasn't guilty? He still had to download their app on it. How else would he keep track of his shakes?

If Sarah went, would he kill her, too? She thought about the pool again, Cassie imagining vanishing. *Without* her daughters, though. Curiosity killed the cat, and Sarah directed the Camry toward Cassie's house. It was dark. She couldn't tell if Derek's truck was in the garage, so she held her head high and just walked into the house, keying in the code, like she always had.

Sarah opened her mouth to call out to Derek, then let it close again. The house didn't feel right. The pepper spray she carried in her purse seemed a thousand miles away and ineffective. She thought of some of the Serenity women who carried guns in their purses, women who went to the range and who weren't ever scared.

"Sarah," Derek's voice sounded more like a croak. Her glance caught the gleaming silver of the knives in the butcher block, but she didn't reach for one. "I found something and it doesn't make sense." He seemed to appear out of nowhere. He wore gray sweatpants, his chest and feet were bare. On each shoulder, one of the girls' footprints was inked, images taken from their birth certificates. A tribal band wound around his bicep, and an eagle in shades of gray shrieked from his left pectoral muscle. All of his body fat seemed to have melted away. *That's Serenity,* Sarah thought proudly. The weight loss contorted the tattoos ever so slightly, making them seem not quite right.

He passed her on the way to the fridge, pulled out a vanilla shake in a plastic bottle, and cracked the top.

"Come with me to the basement."

She watched him drink the shake. Although it sounded like she was agreeing to something out of a horror movie, she said, "Alright."

Sarah knew Cassie grew up in West Virginia. Sarah grew up in Massachusetts. Basements back east were nightmares, cobwebs and stone, dirt floors and musty smells. Root cellars.

Here, Derek flicked a switch and bright track lighting illuminated the room before them. A TV room/playroom, covered in pink toys. A door beyond led to the boiler and Derek's workout room, concrete floored with mats and machines. He led her to the couch, and pulled back a fleece blanket, pink with snowflakes.

She swallowed past a lump in her throat. A husk. As though a creature shed its skin. Maybe a creature weighing thirty-something pounds. One with corn silk blond hair. Sarah brought her fingernail to her mouth, felt her manicure, and resisted the urge to bite down.

"Did you give the girls a shake?"

Never shake a baby, the Serenity Docent told them with a smile, from day one. *And never give a baby one of our shakes. They're not optimized for growing and developing brains and bodies. We don't even think teenagers should have them. Serenity is a special kind of oxidation maximization and muscle building, and it's best for adults.* Marissa and her team drilled this into them from day one. Did you give a baby whiskey? Beer? Heck no! So you never would give them a Serenity shake, even though they came in tasty flavors.

"They wanted to be like Daddy."

Cassie must have a shit a brick. "Is that Arwen?" The younger girl.

"You won't believe me."

Sarah hardened then. "Just tell me. You didn't just give it to her once, did you?"

"She liked it."

"How long, Derek?"

Cassie had been out of town for a week, ironically at the Serenity conference in Palm Springs. Sarah'd had a blast. Cassie seemed distracted.

"A week. Maybe a little more."

"Every day? Both girls? Where's Miri?"

"Cassie has them."

"Where?"

"She screamed at me. Fought me. Told me I was a bad father. We put the girls in a suitcase, and I put them all in my truck when I left for work."

Sarah flashed on the grainy video she'd seen of Derek loading his work truck, caught in the corner of the feed from the guy across the street's security camera. Derek left, and the guy—Peter, she thought his name was—called Maxwell back. Said he thought Derek seemed nervous, that he didn't usually park his truck there. Maxwell played it cool, even defended the husband, asking Peter to think of what he'd gone through.

"Dude ain't acting right."

"We'll talk later," Maxwell had said, glancing at Sarah.

Now, she stared at Derek. "Why are you telling me this?"

"You get the Serenity. I have to bring them some."

Sarah froze. She thought this was a confession. Had imagined bodies dumped in one of the old mine shafts littering the west.

Giving the Serenity product to kids was forbidden. It was day-one stuff. There was no reason to go over why you didn't give it to kids because you just didn't, and the younger the kid, all the more reason you didn't give it. There was a woman in New York who did, and Sarah thought she remembered the toddler didn't survive. The woman was exiled from the Serenity community, and she'd been extremely successful. She had a big, black Serenity Hummer and there was a video on YouTube of it being taken from her.

Would you give Jack Daniel's to a toddler? Does that make Jack Daniel's mysterious and unethical? This from a video, C-list celebrity Marion Dubois, soap star from the '90s, and now spokeswoman for Serenity. *This is an adult drink for adult enhancement and enjoyment.* End of story, Sarah often thought. She didn't have kids of her own, so she didn't think about them much.

"Why?"

"She kept asking!" Derek whined.

"Are they dead?" She thought of the toddler in New York. But Derek had said they needed to bring them some…she was so confused. And she'd seen the…husk…of the little girl.

"They're not fucking dead. They're changing. And we can't let anyone see where they've gone. If someone sees them, they're not coming home."

"Derek, you're speaking in riddles."

"You sell this shit. You know exactly what I'm talking about."

But she didn't. And she didn't sell the stuff per se, she mostly was good at finding beautiful younger women who would be really good at selling a fitness product that was a *commitment.* Women who asked too many questions about Serenity didn't stick around for very long. Don't give it to kids, and don't stop taking it, track your usage on the app to make sure you never miss a dose. That was the long and short of it, and the forever part was what led to really strong downlines.

Led to Sarah's condo. Trips twice a year all over the world and a summer conference. The screening to sell was vast, an honor to be selected. They didn't like that Sarah didn't drink it, but she'd proven herself.

"I don't know what it does. It's a health shake."

"Bullshit!" he screamed in her face and she recoiled.

"Of course it is. You look great. Both of you."

"Cassie," he panted with anger, "does not look great right now. She's changing."

"Where is she? Stop talking in circles, goddammit!" She blew out a deep breath. It was supposed to be calming.

There was a phone number to call for emergencies. Sarah heard it, announced at the beginning and end of each of their meetings, but never gave it much thought. Emergencies, okay. She imagined some of the newer girls struggling to make payments. Something like that.

Derek looked furious with her, and somehow disappointed. "Do you have more of the shakes?"

She shook her head. "I don't—"

"I only have one left. I need more." He paused. Pacing. Thinking. "We have to go to them. Can't let the neighbors video record you getting in the truck. Can't make it look suspicious though. Just…drive away and meet me in the back corner of the Walmart parking lot."

Sarah wanted to say no. Wanted to go home and burrow into bed. But Cassie and the girls were…if not okay, alive, and if they were alive, there was hope. So why wasn't he bringing them to a hospital? Part of the charm of Serenity was that it made people feel *so good* there was never a reason to stop using it. They had testimonials from multiple octogenarians saying they'd been a happy Serenity customer since 2007, with no intention of stopping. "They can bury me with a bottle of Serenity in my hand!" one spunky, fit grandma told the camera.

Downlines

Sarah put her head down and tried to look normal as she went to her car. She drove past a shiny silver cruiser a block away. The glow of a laptop lit the officer's face, but she caught him lifting his head and watching her. With two missing little girls, this case was high priority, and the cops seemed to be doing a good job.

She saw taillights, Derek driving off in the opposite direction. This wouldn't be the only cop watching them tonight. Sure enough, Sarah's phone rang. The same, tired, harried-sounding woman cop. "You both just left."

"Yeah. He's upset."

"Tell me everything."

The throat threatened to close. She reminded herself to breathe. It's mandatory. "He's like a ghost in the house. He's devastated. There's a lot of nastiness online, her phone keeps going off, lots of mean messages on Facebook about her. I told him about her saying she might just leave someday, and he asked me to leave, said he needed to clear his head for a while."

"Huh. He didn't say anything…nothing you felt was suspicious?"

"He sounded hurt. And he said he had to get out of the house, and he was worried you guys would follow him."

"Of course we're going to follow him. Make sure you're someplace safe, we've got it from here."

"Let me know?" she said.

"We'll be in touch tomorrow."

Sarah, a self-respecting single woman in 2019, consumed a lot of true crime. The husband always did it, and killers often went back to visit the bodies. He was going to lead the police right to whatever he wanted to show her. He'd indicated they weren't dead, but weren't okay. What did that mean? Where the hell was Cassie? She groped for any bit of knowledge she possessed about having and shaking a police tail, but there didn't seem to be anyone out on the road. A few cars passed in the other direction, but as far as she could tell, no one followed her. If the police weren't monitoring their phones now (she was hazy on both the legality of doing that, and if they could just do it anyway) they certainly would be able to pull a record of all the texts. Was there a clever text she could send to his new phone (which was super suspicious!) and let him know he was being followed that wouldn't look incriminating as hell?

She got to Walmart, and because it was open twenty-four hours, she went in. She bought a box of tampons because maybe the police wouldn't ask about it. She trudged across the parking lot, back to her car, parked under a streetlight. Well, that'd been dumb, but there are certain trainings that can't be shaken from a person.

A Nevada State Police car rolled past a row over and Sarah's heart pounded inside her chest, hammering constantly. The officer parked, got out, and strolled to the store. He came out five minutes later with a cup of coffee and went about his way.

She'd almost dozed off in the driver's seat when an old red F-150 backed into the spot next to her, the passenger door lined up with her own. "Get in," Derek said. "Leave your phone."

He was right, of course, but letting the device fall from her fingers, then tucking it tight between the seat and center console chewed at her. The truck smelled like stale cigarette smoke, and soda cans and beer bottles almost filled the passenger foot well. She found a spot to tuck her expensive flats. Stolen or borrowed? She didn't want to know. The less she knew the better.

They didn't linger in the Walmart parking lot. In the passenger seat, Sarah chewed adjacent to a gel-polished nail in a way she hadn't for a long time. To the east, the horizon took on a purple cast. She bit through the top layer of skin, and pulled back a small strip despite knowing it would draw blood.

Downlines

She sucked at it, tasting its copper redness. All of this was a mistake. She should be at home, in bed, her phone off. When her best friend wasn't missing, she put her phone on silent from eleven to seven, always with the assumption that if someone had an emergency, there was nothing she could do about it. She didn't have the skills, or knowledge, to help with anything serious and if someone close to her were dead, shouldn't she get one last night of unbroken sleep before learning about it in the morning?

Cassie's disappearance made her feel so proactive. Calling the police, calling Derek. *She* was the one who discovered a crisis, that something was wrong. She was important. Last night, when her phone automatically switched into Do Not Disturb mode, she'd pulled it back. She itched for it. Most adults say they're not addicted to the little boxes, but the things are designed to give jolts of dopamine, and humans crave that. He'd been smart to make her leave it. She could see herself posting on Facebook, location services on. A selfie with Derek in the background, caption: "Anything for Cassie!" It would have gotten a lot of likes. All those clever little apps, always watching and always keeping tabs on people. Honestly, she wasn't sure what she would do without the help.

The truck rattled as Derek pulled off the pavement and onto twin ruts illuminated by the headlights. The purple horizon was behind them now, taking on a distinctly pink caste. She'd cancelled all of today's meetings yesterday. She knew she'd be useless, after three hours of sleep she thanked her past self for this gift. When she got home, she'd take a long shower and lie on the couch. Phone off. There was nothing she could do. If whatever this was didn't help, there was nothing she could do. Maybe she'd leave town for a while.

By the time Derek stopped the truck, the desert around them was gray in a pre-dawn light. A few flowers popped on some of the hearty desert plants, and the truck sat close to a hillside jutting up and out of sight.

In the undercurrent of Sarah's thoughts, she wondered if she would be leaving this place. It hadn't occurred to her to be afraid for herself. This was Derek after all, her best friend's husband. With his face lit only from the green glow of the console, she wasn't so sure.

"Come on." The first he'd spoken since they left the Walmart parking lot.

She did. Ballet flats were not ideal for the terrain. Oh well. He led her down a steep embankment, to a culvert, a smooth round tube of concrete. If it rained, which didn't seem an imminent threat, this culvert would fill with water and drown anyone inside. Shouldn't this type of thing have a grate over the front, to keep people and animals out?

She realized it did, and that some enterprising soul had taken it, and pushed it back, deeper into the culvert. Didn't do much for flash flooding, but it made a makeshift holding cell. Useful as long as things stayed dry.

Derek pulled it back, making a door. "They're in there."

She hesitated, and he passed her a flashlight. Something rustled in the darkness, and a smell wafted to her that reminded her of catching garter snakes when she was a girl. They would mess on her hand to try and get free and leave a musky smell.

"Tell me what's going on." Sarah tried to sound commanding, but it came out small and weak. Derek shoved her, and *oh fuck* dragged the grate back into place. It couldn't have been in there super tight, maybe she could kick it free, maybe she could…

The gate wasn't the issue here in the dark culvert.

A slippery rustle from behind her made her suck her breath in. She didn't want to turn around, she didn't want to look. She thought again of the red emergency 1-800 number printed on every bottle of Serenity.

Sarah turned around.

———

The figure seated before her was unmistakably Cassie. Sarah cried out, both of her hands pressed to her lips. She spun again, rattling the makeshift cage, then back, needing to keep her eyes on the thing in the darkness with her. Someone—Derek—had thrown a handful of glowsticks on the floor and they illuminated the culvert in artificial light, cast long shadows, distorted everything. Something small wriggled at Cassie's feet, and Sarah realized she held a limp shape. A shape the vague mass of a missing three-year-old, clutched to her chest. Her scaly chest.

The vision grounded Sarah. The shed skin at the suburban house gave her an inkling of what to expect, but seeing her friend and her daughters covered in scales battered against her perception of reality. *Lizard people!* she kept thinking ludicrously.

"Hungry," Cassie moaned. The lump in her arms—Arwen it must have been—didn't move. Miri prowled at her feet. The transformation for the children was even more dramatic, which is why every Serenity Curator was trained from day one to *never shake a baby*. Sarah thought the all-natural blend would have been toxic for children, might hospitalize them, kill them…but…

"Derek!" Sarah needed to get out of here.

Cassie's gaze darted in the low light. A light pebbling shone through her brow bones, and they looked to protrude more. Her brown eyes were paler than usual, the pupil reduced to a slit. Her lips were still hers, though. "Derek?"

"Derek!" Sarah cried again. "She's calling for you!"

He wouldn't get close to the bars, but spoke to Cassie without looking at either woman. "You're hungry. I brought *her!*"

It all clicked then. Should have the moment she got in the car with him, or at least when the metal grating closed behind her. She wasn't helping Derek, or rather, she wasn't helping him save Cassie. "Derek, she needs Serenity. I don't know what the babies need." She wasn't sure anything could help Arwen, but she kept that to herself.

"I can get you the shakes!"

"You said you didn't have any."

"I don't but I'm a Curator! I can talk to my downlines, or Marissa." Marissa was their upline, Serenity Mother to both Sarah and Cassie. She didn't want to involve her, but she would. There was also the 800 number on the bottle.

"I'll help you! I already said I would help you when I saw the skin in the basement! Why would you *feed me to her!*"

Derek started to cry, and Miri latched onto Sarah's leg with stubby little arms. The changes moved faster in the children, the flesh and bones more malleable with age. Miri opened her mouth wide to bite—Sarah saw baby teeth replaced with bony ridges of teeth in the roof of her mouth, shining in the yellow light. She wanted to kick the little monster away but instead reached for her, took hold of her, and picked her up. Only forty pounds or so, heavy but manageable even when she squirmed. In Sarah's arms she could keep the child's face pointed in the opposite direction. "Miri, it's auntie Sarah!" Miri stank of a strange blend of mammal and reptile, to the point it made Sarah want to gag. Her skin was cooler than it should have been. Miri should have been sunning herself on a rock, not here in the cold dark.

"Derek, let me out, we can find them something else to eat. I'll help you. I don't want to hurt your family."

The metal grated, and sobbing Derek yanked her back, helping to push the child back into the gloom.

Sarah wanted to scream as he pushed the grate back. To cry. Wash her hands. Run from here. Miri battered herself against the metal while Cassie sat silent, cradling her daughter and watching.

"I didn't mean to," Derek said.

Sarah swallowed past the helpless rage lump in her throat. It didn't matter what he did or did not mean to do. "What time is it?"

"Four thirty," he said.

"What have you tried feeding them?"

Derek exploded at her. "Everything! You think I went straight to bringing you here? McDonald's, raw meat, I killed a fucking sheep and brought it. I brought a live cat, but it clawed at them and escaped. Cassie just keeps telling me I'm wrong, I need to bring her—" his words broke off in a sob.

She stood behind them, against the metal grating. The curves of her human form were there, strange under the pebbly skin. Her generous breasts pressed against the metal bars, and Sarah looked away. "I need live meat. Human meat. If you can't bring me a shake." Her words weren't right, as though her teeth and tongue were changing in her mouth.

Sarah ran through the shake inventory in her head. It was supposed to be a quiet week. She thought she could skate and get more at the next team meeting on Thursday. Marissa was going to be *pissed*. Derek needed it, so he didn't wind up like them. Cassie needed it because it might save her. The girls? Well, she'd focus on Cassie now.

Sarah tried the controlled exhale again, but it wasn't working. "Let's go to the strip. We can find someone there and bring them back to feed her. Then I have to get shakes for her. She needs them. It might stop the transformation. But they're hungry now."

"The strip?"

Sarah loved true crime. Maybe not anymore, now that she was living some semblance of it, but she knew enough about successful killers. Derek would be busted if he took her, his wife's best friend. The husband always did it. If they found someone on the strip… maybe they had a shot.

"Let's go! There are always people on the strip who won't be missed." Tears slid down her cheeks as she said it.

———

She actually dozed off in the truck, her face against the glass, as they rattled over desert and onto the old road. She wondered if the police were watching them even now, if the best thing to do would be to flag down an officer the second she saw one.

What would they do to Cassie? To Miri? Or poor little Arwen? That she'd never heard a serious news story about a…she felt ridiculous calling them lizard people…case like Cassie's scared her. When it was time for your shake, the app told you. You clicked a glossy blue button confirming you'd drank your Serenity (available in vanilla, chocolate, or strawberry, as well as fun seasonal flavors like pumpkin spice and apple pie) and it suddenly dawned on Sarah why location-tracking services were on and why the app was so domineering. It wasn't just targeted ads. She'd always thought it was kind of neat, the way Facebook showed her perfect ads for sweatshirts with cat ears and cute wall hangings that said "plant mom." She'd always assumed people who didn't like it had something to hide. Well, now she had something to hide. And it was about to get a whole lot worse.

Maybe she'd call Marissa in the morning, though wasn't Marissa at a leadership retreat in Costa Rica? No, that was last week. Marissa would know. Sarah expunged the thought from her head as she looked around the truck.

"What?" Derek sounded defensive.

"I'm looking around. We've got to get someone in here to bring back to her. They may not like it."

He opened and closed his mouth.

"I can't believe you were going to feed me to her."

"I was just going to get more shakes from you. You said you didn't have any and I panicked. They're going to nail me for this, and I don't know what Cassie will do."

Sarah knew exactly what Cassie would do if Derek went to jail. "Die in the cage you left her in." Just like Derek would die in the cage he'd be put in.

"I can't let her loose. Miri got out of the house. I had to catch her in the backyard. She's strong."

"I know," Sarah said. "What possessed you to give it to them?"

"They wouldn't leave me alone. I didn't think it would do…this. I didn't think…I thought it would give them a stomachache and teach them a lesson."

"Cassie didn't stress how important it is not to give it to them?"

"I don't need a lecture from you. I can see what I've done. I get it now. Lesson learned, okay?"

"They eat meat?"

"I don't think it's good for Cassie. I think it makes her more…animal. She needs the shakes." Sarah thought of the shake she'd seen Derek drinking yesterday. There was a certain logic in making sure he stayed medicated, if he gave up his remaining shakes to Cassie, who knew what would become of her, and they knew how he would wind up.

"I don't understand why the shakes did it to the kids, and no shakes did it to Cassie."

Sarah did. They didn't spell it out for their Curators, but she got it now. The shakes had too many "nutrients" for small children, and adults would start depending on Serenity's proprietary blend of "nutrients," and could suffer "ill effects," particularly if quitting cold turkey. An abrupt cessation had even been known to result in death. The results were so good that people never stopped. The price point wasn't too high—it didn't need to be. A satisfied customer was a customer for life.

Now it was five and just growing light when they turned onto Las Vegas Boulevard. The strip wasn't deserted—it never was. The pedestrians fell into distinct camps, easily identifiable. First there were the service workers, heading to and from shifts. Heads down, all business. You had the East Coasters, either running (ugh) or so set in their ways that they were already up and sightseeing. These folks were clean and showered, bright eyed and bushy tailed, and ready to begin their days. They'd be unconscious after a few drinks at 7:00 PM. Then there were the folks whose night hadn't ended yet. They were still drinking, still partying, and they, for the most part, looked like hot messes. A woman crying with a broken heel while three other women rallied around her. A group of guys with bleary stares, each holding yard-long drinks.

Lastly there were the homeless folks. Tucked under stairways, against transformer boxes.

"What's your plan?" Derek said.

"Find a way to get one of these people in the truck. But there are cameras everywhere, so we have to be careful."

"I hate this."

But you wanted to feed me to her? She didn't rise to the bait. He'd done it. She shouldn't even be here.

"Homeless guy?" Derek said.

Her heart panged. No, she couldn't do that. One of the partiers. Someone close to blackout drunk. She could make up a story about him about how he deserved it.

"No. Drunk guy."

"Sarah, logistically a drunk chick would be easier."

He was right. Logistically, probably a homeless woman would be easiest of all. Someone they could overpower. And a homeless person wouldn't be missed as quickly. She wanted to be moral, be a *Dexter*-type killer, find someone who deserved it.

But someone they could control would make the whole thing faster and easier. She wanted to tell Derek she hated him, but she couldn't. She was in this as much as he was. It was her idea, to save her own skin.

She thought about the statistics. Some podcasts called them *The Lesser Dead*, runaways, junkies, sex workers, people the world had already given up on. Many of them didn't even have anyone out there looking for them, had never been reported missing.

"There." Derek pointed.

A woman huddled under a pedestrian overpass, slight, with messy brown hair. Sarah's first instinct: *If we cleaned her up, with those cheekbones, she'd be a perfect Serenity Curator.* She huddled with a blanket over her shoulders—Las Vegas nights get cold—holding a sign that said "Homeless, anything helps." Sarah looked from Derek and back to herself. They both had the appearance of harmless suburbanites, nothing about either one of them suggested murderers.

"Go get her," Sarah said.

"We both know it'll be easier if you do it."

He was right, but she didn't want to admit it, and played dumb. "Why's that?"

Derek gave her a look. "She'll trust you. Come on, if some dude approaches you, you'd freak out. But if a woman came up to you…?"

He was right and she didn't like it one bit. She was about to be a traitor to her entire gender. The part of her brain that had never see a lizard person argued: she lifted other women up, got them good jobs, helped them excel at their jobs. Nikki'd just passed her in revenue and Curators recruited. That's what Serenity was, a way to empower women: to look their best and to be their best. Her whole life she'd been good for women, it was only now, for one night that she needed to go against her instincts.

She got out of the truck. Derek yelped behind her. He didn't follow.

She wanted to shout at the dirty woman—Cassie would surely want better than this, but beggars can't be choosers. Cassie huddled, trapped in a culvert craving human flesh. The culvert worried her, too. She hadn't looked at the forecast since yesterday, but if rain came, they'd have three fewer problems to worry about.

"Hey," Sarah made her voice sweet as saccharine, like she was talking to one of her downlines during their first few months, when it was really hard, and they realized that most of their Facebook friends weren't actually their friends. The woman looked up. Big blue eyes. "You okay?" Wow, dumb question.

"I mean…yeah? I guess? But I don't have anything to eat and my boyfriend kicked me out. He kept our cat."

She sounded a little high, which made Sarah's job easier, but the detail about the cat just about killed her. It didn't matter if the guy had a good reason or not, you don't keep a woman's cat.

In this case, though, it was for the best that he did, as this young woman wouldn't be able to take care of her cat for much longer. Or maybe that wasn't a new thing and it was why he did it. It made Sarah feel better to think that she was a bad cat mom. She decided in her imagination this woman had even gone so far as to have the cat declawed.

"We've got food if you want to come with us." Sarah sounded like some kind of a sex maniac with a van bragging about puppies or candy. "I mean we can take you. Drive thru. What do you want?"

Would the woman taste better to Cassie if they fed her first?

"Why?"

"I have a friend in a lot of trouble right now, and helping you feels like the best way to help her."

The woman's face softened. "You'd take me to get food?"

"Yeah, come on."

The woman started to pack up her stuff. "What's wrong with your friend?"

"Withdrawal," Sarah said. "Rough stuff."

"I know what that's like," the woman said. All her belongings fit in a backpack, and they headed toward the red truck. Sarah kept expecting the woman to balk and run, to decide this was, in fact, sketchy as fuck. But she didn't. Sarah climbed in, sitting in the middle, and the woman hopped in beside her.

"This is my husband Derek. Where do you want to go?"

Derek glared at her when she said husband, but it was quick.

"I'm Katie," she replied, so close to Cassie it made Sarah recoil. "Can we just go to McDonald's?"

"Sure thing," Derek said, and off they went. He slipped something into her Diet Coke, and after she'd eaten two egg sandwiches and two hash browns, she was out, head drooped on the door. Sarah plucked the soda from her hand before she spilled it.

They didn't speak on the drive back to the culvert. Sarah, in the middle seat, pressed against Derek, finding his muscled leg warm and unpleasant. She thought again about how if it rained, Cassie and her daughters would be wiped out. Would that be the best thing? The kindest thing?

In daylight, the red truck looked incredibly conspicuous against all the shades of brown in the earth. Sarah kept looking around, scanning the sky for drones, helicopters. Did Katie have a phone someone could use to track her?

No one cared to track a woman who hadn't even been able to keep a cat. The dirt on the skin on her neck, the grime under her fingernails, it all spoke of someone who'd been forgotten. Good for them, not so good for Katie. Maybe not good for Cassie, if she didn't taste good, but beggars can't be choosers.

Well, tonight she wouldn't be looking for a handout or a place to sleep. They'd send her off with a full stomach.

It struck Sarah again that she could have made a Serenity Curator out of her. Was this how she ought to make amends when this was over with Cassie? Talk to the homeless women on the strip and recruit from there? It would be great publicity for Serenity, and she'd likely find some motivated sellers. She wasn't so sure about Serenity at the moment, though. Not sure at all. So much so, that she couldn't go there right now, couldn't fathom the apparent depravity of the beloved company often unfairly labeled as a pyramid scheme.

As they descended into darkness, Katie asleep (unconscious) in Derek's arms, Sarah thought it might be time to look for a new job.

Cassie hissed at them. Miri snarled. Arwen, like before, lay still in Cassie's arms. Sarah wondered if the girl was dead, or if a meal of fresh meat could revive her. They'd find out.

Downlines

Sarah stood and watched as Derek set Katie down. Cassie snarled and rushed at the metal grate. In the end, Derek slid it open and kicked at his family as he pushed the unconscious woman inside. At least it distracted them so he could close the grate. Sarah didn't feel the need to bear witness. She walked back into the sunlight as the crunching and tearing sounds started. No screams. That was something.

In the growing Nevada heat, she sunk against a rock. She should cry. She should feel something other than tired and dimly annoyed, concerned about how she'd get back to her car and apartment and explain to the police why her car and her phone spent the night in a Walmart parking lot. She had to go to Marissa to get more Serenity and had to post a Facebook Live video later in the afternoon to inspire all her downlines to keep up the hustle and #findcassie.

Derek didn't speak to her when he came out into the light, squinting at the sun. He'd aged a decade overnight, she saw, and his eyes were watery. He hadn't slept and she didn't think the police would like the way he looked. She tried to memorize where they were, so if he got arrested, she could come back, and…and what? Set Cassie free?

"Did Arwen eat?" Sarah had to ask, about halfway back to Walmart.

"I'm pretty sure the change killed her. Cassie won't let me look. Put her down to eat, but scooped her back up again immediately," his voice breaking.

"Do we need a story for the cops?"

He paused and Sarah almost asked the question a second time. "The truth?"

"No!" It came out sharper than she wanted. "I'm going to see Marissa. I need to get you both more shakes."

"I've got one left."

"Okay, I'll have more for you."

"If I get arrested—" He left it unspoken. Probably designer protein shakes weren't on the prison menu. She pictured Cassie, her flat stomach lined with creamy scales. Would the cops tase him? Beat him? Send him to a lab for dissection?

"They want me to take a polygraph. I can't pass it. They want me there at two."

"Polygraphs are garbage." Sarah had listened to enough true crime podcasts to know that. "Can you say your lawyer doesn't want you to do one?"

"I don't have a lawyer."

Marissa. Sarah doubted this was the first time this scenario had played out. "You can't take a polygraph and you can't go back in there without a lawyer."

"They'll think I'm guilty."

"They already do."

"I fucked up. I fucked it all up. When I close my eyes, I see their faces."

"Me, too."

"You didn't see them eating."

"Stop. What do we tell the cops?"

"You came over, we fought, I couldn't sleep so I went for a drive, got tired and fell asleep in the Walmart parking lot."

"Why did we fight?"

"You've never thought I was good enough for her."

Sarah opened and closed her mouth. Now wasn't the time for bullshit. He wasn't wrong. She was also mildly embarrassed that with the weight he'd lost on Serenity, she'd started rethinking her assessment. "What about me?"

"You're not a suspect and I bet they're not tracking you. You were home, sleeping."

He was probably right. It was probably a safe lie, but it was so easy to prove with camera footage and phone pings. "I hate this," she said.

"You're not…if they arrest me… I'm going to turn into one of those things."

"I'm going straight to Marissa, going to figure out what we do." Sarah thought up the line, over Marissa's head. Lance? All the way to founder Mark Morris?

Derek shook his head. He dropped her at the Walmart doors, and Sarah went in, bought some sunglasses and a floppy hat (like that would help). By then her fingers itched for her phone, to see what had happened, who'd messaged her. She couldn't remember the last time she'd gone this long without it. It was pathetic, a grown woman so addicted to a small computer box.

The inside of her car radiated heat as she opened the door, and she lingered a moment with it open before she slid inside. She wondered where the cameras were, if they were picking her up even now. It didn't matter. She hated that Derek hadn't wanted to put together a story, hated that he would probably wind up in jail and the transformation would befall him.

Criminals didn't drink Serenity, it was part of their brand, to focus only on upstanding citizens, *good* people, and only now Sarah realized she didn't know what the fuck it meant. Except she did—they couldn't give this drink to someone who was going to wind up in jail. The messaging was so ingrained, so drilled into them, they didn't question it. They were told who their ideal clients were and then to go forth and prosper. Her breath hitched in her chest as it all made so much more sense. She finally picked up her phone once the blowers on the car got a handle on the Nevada heat. Nothing.

No messages. No one reaching out, not even the police. She wondered about taking the battery out, the SIM card out, but decided it was more important to have her phone. She went to social media, as there was always activity there. *Find Cassie, bring Cassie home.* But then a bunch of darker things. Cassie

Freidman was asking for it. *Have you seen her videos? The way she bullies her husband? No wonder he killed her. A fine man like that can only be pussy whipped for so long.*

Sarah had a particular loathing of the term "pussy whipped," as with most women of an age, it had been applied to her as the whipper, and as with most women it was complete and total domineering bullshit. There was a reason there was no man in her life. No one would accuse her of that shit again.

Cassie's account sat dormant, no one moderating the comments, Marissa wouldn't like that. *Or maybe she would.* Is there such thing as bad publicity? Cassie lived her life on social media; she said she didn't want anything getting in the way of her connecting with her clients, curators, and potential new curators. So she tolerated vile messages in her inbox, propositions, pictures of men's anatomy, women telling her how to mother her children better. Because she laid herself bare here, they savaged her. And in her disappearance the gloves were off.

I worked with her for, like, a minute. As admin assistant. What. A. Bitch. She wanted a nanny and a gopher. I wanted to learn about her business. UGH. Sarah remembered Kairi. She'd been an entitled Gen Z brat, constantly snapping selfies. Kairi ruined a pair of jeans...kneeling in a puddle of child excrement. That was the end of that working relationship.

"Bitch," Sarah muttered.

She clicked on the last video Cassie ever posted, from the morning before she went missing. It had many more comments than her usual post, and as predicted, they ran the gamut. Sarah turned the volume up.

Cassie, cleaning up her home. She had a bandana wrapped around her hair, looking super cute, immaculate makeup, and her long nails were done in a glittery pink manicure. She held the camera away from her—clients and Curators had to see how she'd lost almost twenty pounds since she started with Serenity, needed to see the how her baby bump somehow made her look even more petite. The black shirt was low cut and accentuated her boobs. If you got 'em, Cassie always said, flaunt 'em. Sarah didn't really have them, and didn't do nearly as many videos. She never managed the confidence. Cassie started all her videos with a genial "Hey guys!" that made you feel like it was just the two of you talking.

The comments from when she'd first gone live were all positive. Lots of talk about adding a third baby to the family, lots of talk about already having a third baby in caring for husband Derek. Cassie picking up his underwear with a smirk. "He's in his gym right now doing pushups," she told the world. "I created a monster when I introduced him to Serenity." Sarah had watched this video live, of course. Her own "Yass girl!" and "lol" and "Go get them!" comments floated past, but Cassie's phrasing turned her already-sour stomach. How long had it been since she'd eaten? Cassie continued. "But guys, you've seen the before pictures." She turned her camera on a framed wedding photo. Cassie and Derek, arms around each other, smiling. Each one much heavier. "He saw my journey with Serenity after Arwen was born, and finally jumped on the wagon with me. It's so amazing having a partner who's actually investing in himself."

Sarah read the comments from after the news broke: "He invested in himself alright. By giving this bitch what she deserved!" "God, she's so condescending. So glad I never have to hear her voice again."

Sarah thought of the rasping words from Cassie. This commenter, like she didn't have the power to just unfollow? How could people be so cruel?

She drove home, watching her mirrors for a police tail, for the cops to jump out at her. Nada. Good. She expected a black-

and-white cruiser in her driveway, or more insidiously something undercover, but saw none of that either.

To see Marissa, she needed to be at her best. She showered, choked down a cup of yogurt, and did her makeup. Big and bold, cat eye liner, some sparkle. She slid on some stylishly torn denim shorts, sandals with Swarovski crystals that caught the light, and a plain black top. Marissa talked a big game about her door being always open, about any of her Curators being welcome, but Sarah never felt confident to take her up on it. She always treated Sarah like she was special, but she did that with everyone, which meant Sarah wasn't special at all. Sarah was aloof and wary of Marissa's perpetual bubbliness. Never mean to anyone. Cassie had her persona, but she shed it for her real friends. Marissa was eternal gratitude and grace, sophisticated and savvy. The veneer never slipped, not even for a moment.

She glanced at her bed, wished she could lie down for a little while. Images of scales popped up in Sarah's mind, the way they curved around Cassie's flesh. She wondered if the police had come for Derek yet. On the way across town, she tried to talk herself out of what she'd seen. There had to be another explanation, the health shakes she sold couldn't fundamentally alter a person's biology, anatomy…whatever it took to take a healthy woman and children and change them into reptilian monsters. Cannibalistic reptilian monsters. It wasn't possible.

Marissa lived in a giant new house, like almost everyone in the area. They'd gone up by the dozens with very little personality other than size. Its faux stone façade was more impressive from the curb than up close, and little lizards skittered out of Sarah's way. She felt like she should have brought a gift, an offering. Something. She wracked her brain to remember if Marissa was or was not drinking this month, but since she hadn't brought an offering, she supposed it didn't matter. Her visit here wasn't pageantry, she needed help.

Downlines

Sarah tugged at the frayed fringe on her shorts and rang the bell. A camera watched her, and she did her best to smile and stop fidgeting. An overbearing mother and aunt would have been proud. She kept one denim lint ball between her manicured fingers and rolled it back and forth, back and forth. The sun drummed down on her, and pools of sweat started to blossom under her arms and pooled between her breasts. There was a sound within the house, and for a hot second Sarah imagined one of the lizard things opening the door, hissing at her, consuming her.

Instead, a short Guatemalan woman stood before her in a pink maid's outfit, looking both ridiculous and classy all at the same time. The ostentatiousness of the foyer slapped her, three stories, grand sweeping staircases that would have been more at home at Tara (the first fine home that sprang to Sarah's imagination). The faux southwestern theme with tans and turquoise and coral was tired, and the room carried no personality or flare. The only statement it managed to make was "I am large and cost a lot of money." Good for Marissa, Sarah supposed.

"*Bienvenido,*" she said without much inflection.

Sarah stepped into the air-conditioning, reveling in how it washed her body. Those pools of sweat turned almost instantly to ice and she repressed a shiver.

"I'd like to see Marissa, please."

"You are?"

"Sarah Perrin," she said with a smile.

"Serenity girl?"

"Yeah," she replied, but couldn't muster much enthusiasm for it.

"This way."

Sarah glanced into a chef-grade kitchen—stainless appliances immaculate. It didn't give the energy of a space that was used. In contrast, the woman led Sarah to the back of the house, outside, to a poolside oasis. No wonder Marissa didn't come inside. Everything she needed was back here. She lay by the pool letting the sun drench her already-bronze skin. Sarah knew sun worship was wrong but envied her glow. Her black-and-white polka dot bikini was big enough that one couldn't specifically editorialize on its size, but not by much.

The sound of a waterfall almost completely covered the pool pump noise, and palm trees shaded the seating area from the blistering sun.

"*Sarah!*" Her voice was excited but didn't hold much in the way of recognition. She wondered if Marissa could tell her three things about herself. But then, unlike, say, Cassie, Sarah hadn't completely leaned into her personal life to sell Serenity. She didn't have a husband or kids to use for likes on the internet, and she supposed one could pretty easily forget about her.

"What a beautiful garden!"

"This is my happy place for sure. Can I have Conchita get you something to drink? Boozy? Not boozy?"

It wasn't even eleven. "Not boozy would be great."

Marissa barked something in Spanish. Conchita appeared with a sweating glass of what looked like sparkling water. Sarah thanked her for it, and Conchita dematerialized back into the house.

"What's on your mind, Sarah? How's business?"

Good, leading up to the disappearance of my best friend. Haven't given it much thought over the past few days. The unanswered emails nagged at her.

"You know Cassie is missing." Not a question, everyone knew Cassie was missing.

"That poor dear. I heard she took the girls and went home to West Virginia."

"I don't think she did." Sarah steeled herself. "Marissa, what happens if you suddenly stop drinking Serenity?"

"You don't." Marissa's salesey-faux nice demeanor stalled. "That's one of the first things we teach you girls."

"Oh, I know, but what if someone does?"

Marissa's jaw jutted out, ever so slightly. "Do you just need to get them more? I have some in my back room, ready for you to take."

Probably a good idea to get some for Derek.

"I do need more, thank you. But if someone just…stops."

"Why would she do that?"

"Doesn't matter why. What happens?"

"You can't let her."

"Imagine it was out of my control."

"There is a red 1-800 number on the bottle that someone should call for her."

Sarah ground her teeth. "What happens if you call the number?" She'd seen it, of course, on every case she handed over, on the website, but never really paused to think about what happens if it were called.

"I don't know. It's never happened. You're not just a saleswoman, Sarah. You're a coach. You signed on to be a *Curator* for these people and they're not just going to know how to navigate a product as complicated as—"

Sarah tuned Marissa out. She wanted to scream at her that it was her golden girl, it was Cassie, who was trapped in a culvert, not even human anymore.

"What happens if I call the number?" she said again.

"Like I said, Sarah, it's never happened in our region. So I don't know. I've never let one of my flock make such a reckless decision." A glimmer of fear in Marissa's eye suggested this wasn't quite true. Was she picturing scales?

"What about giving it to kids?"

Now Marissa gaped. "You need to refine your screening technique. This person is a danger. You need to call that 1-800 number and do it now. This product is not safe for children and you know it. I'm so disappointed in you."

It wasn't me, it wasn't me, it wasn't me...but not worth saying out loud. Cassie had recruited Sarah, for heaven's sake!

"Thank you." Sarah set the sparkling water, barely touched, on a low table. She wanted to scream *Help me!* but pressed her lips together in a flat line. If Marissa knew what happened to Cassie she could go to the cops, and...Sarah didn't know what would happen, but she didn't trust any of it. She didn't trust Marissa any more. She needed to get out of there. She didn't trust the red 1-800 number, but dialed it the moment she got into her car, hearing the phone ring through the speakers as the air-conditioning vanquished the heat.

She hadn't picked up the shakes.

One half-ring and it devolved into a mechanical fax-like screeching. She mashed her finger on the red button to hang up, her fingernail clicking the glass screen. Tears sprang to her eyes. She wanted to go back and screech at Marissa, her precious 1-800 number was out of service. Sarah tried again with the same results. She hadn't even gotten the extra case of shakes for Derek. No time to cry. She shot Petra a quick text.

HEY GIRL, DO YOU HAVE ANY EXTRA VANILLA SHAKES? I'VE GOT A BUYER WHO WANTS THEM NOW! I'LL BUY THEM OFF YOU!

Vanilla always sold the worst, Serenity's version of vanilla wound up tasting more like chemicals. Sarah cast one more look at Marissa's mansion, dialed the 1-800 number carefully, and when the screeching came through the phone, she wanted to throw it as hard as she could. Instead, she set it gently on the passenger seat and pulled away from the curb. She spent the drive fuming, in her own world, thinking about the unfair position Derek had put them all in, seeing Arwen's limp body.

Would Cassie be...medicated? Captured? Sarah imagined a zookeeper with a net and a tranquilizer gun circling Cassie and Arwen. What was the potential outcome for her here? Was there a happy ending?

She should sleep. Well, sleep as soon as she heard from Petra. And if she didn't hear quickly, she could try Abby or Veruca. If she'd only had the presence of mind to get some off Marissa while she was right there. 1-800 number, her ass.

So this was like, a fluke? The first time Serenity ever caused—

Her thoughts cut off mid flow when she noticed the truck following her. Big. Black. Windows tinted so dark she couldn't even see the shape of the driver. It caught her eye over the last few intersections, but as she pulled off the main road heading for her development, it followed her. She scanned the rest of her rearview mirror, hoping to see a cop car. No dice. Could still be an easy coincidence, of course. Sarah's Spidey-Sense told her it wasn't. The same way she knew Cassie's...change...was connected to Serenity, and maybe not the first time it'd happened. A memory flooded in of her first National Conference, a place of bright neon colors and smiles and Curators from all across America. A moment of silence for a young woman from Florida. Sarah assumed cancer, because everything was cancer, but she'd been caught in the whirlwind, and didn't care about dead women. Second National Conference, if memory served her, had been three smiling faces in the "in memoriam" section. That year she hadn't cared because she and Cassie had been pre-gaming up in the room and their coffee mugs held a vile tropical punch rum drink, equal parts red food coloring, sugar, and booze. The clarity of the memory—Cassie and the punch, being careful not to color their lips red, making sure they didn't act too drunk, even though at least a third of the conference had the same idea.

The buzz of her phone shook her. She pushed the listen button and Petra's text response played through her speakers, read by a robot trying to sound human.

"Oh em gee yes I am home until four o'clock PM if you want to swing by I'm happy you found someone who likes the vanilla yuck."

Sarah glanced at the truck in the mirror and carefully spoke her response back, so the robot would understand. "Awesome. Be over in ten."

She drove past her condo, did a loop in the complex, and headed toward Petra's house.

The black truck followed. Worry increased as she drew closer to Petra's. Petra was a young single mom with two sons. She had a close female friend, and Cassie thought maybe she was in the closet, albeit poorly. Was Sarah putting all of them in danger? Didn't matter, Cassie and Derek needed the shakes. This would buy her time to put in an order for them, and maybe it would put things right. The kids gnawed at her. If they changed because they drank it…well, they weren't drinking it now, so…? And Sarah didn't know much about anatomy, but she wasn't optimistic that a body could just…change back. That said, the idea that a body could turn into one of those things would have seemed impossible a day or so ago. It made her want to cry again. She peered into the rearview as she pulled into Petra's driveway.

The truck was gone.

"Girl, I am *so glad* I could help!" Petra thrust the case of shakes towards her. Sarah took it, glad to have her hands filled. Two little brown faces watched through the living room window and Sarah did her best to waggle her fingers and smile at them.

"Anything about Cassie?"

The question took her off guard. It probably shouldn't have, it was logical, but it hit Sarah just so and all that almost-crying transformed into ragged sobs. "I don't think she's okay," Sarah lied. Of course she wasn't okay.

"Oh my God," Petra said, and gave her an awkward hug around the case of Serenity. "Is it Derek?"

Sarah shook her head. "It can't be…can it?"

"Honey, the husband always does it."

Sarah's wounded look was real. Petra was spot on, of course. "He's a really nice guy."

"You stay away from him. He's poison. Work on business, on you, on finding Cassie and those girls. That guy always gave me the creeps."

Sarah nodded. "She's my best friend and I miss her." Not a lie. Not at all. Re-framing it with that simple sentence made her cry harder. It would all be simpler if Derek just strangled her to death, smothered those babies with pillows. This death sentence was more complicated, and she'd let herself get involved.

She'd killed for them.

The heat was too much. The tears, the beating sun, the memory of the woman (Sarah wouldn't use her name—she couldn't) simply asking for fucking McDonald's.

"Have you slept?"

Sarah shook her head.

"Take your shakes," Petra plucked them from her and walked them to the passenger seat of the car. "Go home, take a rest. The shakes will wait."

"They won't, though. They're going to run out."

A cardinal rule: you don't let your clients run out of product. Petra knew this and gave a little sigh. "One quick drop-off. You look exhausted."

She nodded. She could at least bring them to Derek, let him know she could go with him later. The idea made her shudder. She thought about some friends she'd had in high school with snakes and lizards. They didn't eat every day—that was a mammal thing, for creatures that need to pump warm blood. What even was Cassie now?

It took a moment to reclaim her car from the Nevada heat. The air conditioner fought to cool the space down. Sarah took the time to scan the neighborhood for the black truck. No sign. Maybe she'd been wrong: no correlation between it and the useless 1-800 number, which she tried again to the same effect.

She went to Cassie and Derek's house, knocked three times before using her key to let herself in. Derek wasn't there—was he at work, with Cassie, or had he been arrested? She put four shakes in the fridge, and the rest in the pantry. The fridge was mostly bare—something that never would have happened on Cassie's watch. Did Derek know, would he get takeout somewhere? She couldn't see him stopping at the grocery store. The emptiness of the house shook her. Drinks after work, playing with the kids, but mostly Cassie's videos, her Instagram stories, made Sarah and anyone else who wanted to feel like family. Sarah knew all about needing to jiggle the handle to the upstairs toilet, about the time a squirrel ran in through the patio door and sent Cassie and Derek on a wild chase, as the girls squealed in delight.

Cassie was going to have another baby. It seemed impossible now. She wasn't a doctor, she didn't know exactly what was going on, didn't know if Cassie could be saved. She'd miscarried so many times already—three—and women across the country lauded her for her openness, her willingness to talk about the taboo subject of her rainbow babies. Derek hated it.

There had to be a balance, though. When Sarah heard he found out about the second miscarriage because a coworker's wife saw it on Facebook, she said something to Cassie—that was awful; disrespectful to Derek.

Cassie's face went blank.

Oh shit, Sarah thought. *I've overstepped.*

"Why didn't he pick up his phone then? Why wasn't he at the doctor's with me? Why didn't he respond to any of my texts? I'm not even sure he gives a fuck about me. I tried calling him. I needed someone to hear me. I needed everyone to hear me, after that."

The words lingered with Sarah. "Fuck you, Derek," she said out loud.

Why had he given the shakes to the girls? His actions put all of this in motion.

She felt icky after saying it, those words bouncing around the empty house. She got out as quickly as possible. This time she'd kept the car running and sunk into the blissful cool. Home. Sleep. Cassie could wait.

Or could she?

Sarah argued with herself. She *needed* to sleep, needed to eat, too. The moment her stomach registered as hungry, though, she smelled a phantom fragrance of McDonald's. The hunger twisted into a sour sensation. Sleep first. Just a nap. Then…who knew what came next. Maybe Derek would text that he'd taken care of everything, thank her for the help last night, and it would be over. Cassie would call as soon as she felt better, and the secret would go with them to the grave. *But was it too late for the unborn baby and for Arwen? What about Miri?*

She pulled into her own lot and hurried inside, carrying the last case of shakes. The air-conditioning hummed, and other than that, her condo felt lifeless. Not even a houseplant. No responsibility for anything but herself.

And her downlines, of course. They were hers to fuss over. But here? In the condo? Nothing.

With less and less optimism she tried the 1-800 number again, to the same fax machine squealing result. She didn't want to text Derek, but had to. He needed to know she'd dropped off the shakes.

DROPPED OFF CASSIE'S SERENITY ORDER. VANILLA, RIGHT? PRAYING FOR YOU BOTH

Clasped hands emoji, heart emoji.

Gagging emoji, Sarah thought.

She sunk onto her bed, a white down comforter reaching up for her and embracing her.

And then, just as her eyes closed, a knock on the door. Authoritative. Scary. Not the police, if knowledge gained from thousands of hours of television was to be believed. This somehow was…worse.

It never occurred to Sarah not to answer, to stay silent as a mouse in her bedroom until the danger passed. She paused at her mirror—habit, she didn't even think about it, dragged a brush through her hair, and went to the door.

A woman pushed into her home. Sarah gaped at her. She was something from an action movie, not a real person, impossible.

The woman's age was indecipherable, skin weathered. Sarah thought of her Rodan Fields sales kit in the bedroom— this woman needed sun protection and moisturization, stat. Funny Sarah registered that before the woman's missing eye, or the jagged scar that pulled the right side of her lip up into a sneer. The military cut of her pants and vest, the cap holding back a graying ponytail. Very Linda Hamilton.

"You have the wrong house," Sarah said. Of course she didn't. Sarah wasn't stupid, but a stubborn part of her brain clung desperately to *normal*, and Sarah of forty-eight hours ago would never have a reason to interact with a woman like this.

"You called the number. Over and over, you called the number."

Sarah opened her mouth and closed it again. The woman spoke with an accent. Russian? Sarah wasn't good with things like this. Somewhere over there, she imagined a dark swath of the globe where she wasn't able to identify countries on a map.

She wanted to speak but didn't know what words to use.

Then the woman pulled a gun. Some small guns look like cartoons, silly. This one looked cruel and equally able to inflict violence as its larger brethren. Sarah's breath caught in her throat, and she couldn't get air. There was no longer air in the room, she couldn't breathe.

"Please don't hurt me." It came out as a pathetic squeak.

"You called me."

Sarah's brain started to regain some of its function. She bobbed her head once. Yes, she called. Her lungs seemed less agreeable, the world tightening to a pin hole, all centered on the tight round barrel of the little gun. Her chest fought its normal expansions.

The woman rolled her eyes and used the gun to point at the sofa. "Sit, breathe."

She sat. She pictured Derek on TV, begging for his family back. There wasn't anyone to beg for her. Cassie, once. She thought of lizard-Cassie at a press conference, her voice hissing. She laughed and the stranger slapped her.

The slap could have been harder, and it did kickstart her lungs working again. *That was a panic attack,* she thought. She'd never actually had one before.

"You called. Why?"

Sarah brought her hands to her eyes and rubbed, aware mascara, eye liner, eyeshadow, and Bye Bye Undereye were all smearing and sliding everywhere. She pressed into her skull. She could lie. She could say it was a mistake. A broken phone.

A joke. She wanted to see what happened. Any number of excuses. This female Rambo wouldn't buy any of them. If she lied…this woman might hurt her. Sarah had never been hurt. Never even really been scared before last night.

"My friend stopped drinking the shakes. Her husband gave it to their daughters. I don't know how to help her."

"Your friend is Cassiopeia, the missing woman?"

She nodded. "What happened to her? I don't understand!" What if the woman didn't know what she was talking about?

"How many daughters?"

"Two. Last I saw them, one of them…I don't know if she was all right."

"Take me to them."

"You can help her? Cure her and the children?"

The woman nodded. Help her, yes…Sarah looked again at the gun and wondered what helping her meant. She didn't like it. "The husband. Call him there, too."

"I think he has to work—"

She cut Sarah off. "This is his wife. More important than work. Call him, and if you tell him anything funny, I'll shoot you."

The rock in the pit of her empty stomach swirled and tumbled. "You need me to find her?"

She shook her head once. "While you visited your friend, I put a tracker on his truck."

He's too smart to take his own truck out there, to the culvert. But was he? Derek was tired, and obviously not very smart to begin with, or he wouldn't have started them all down this path.

"It's better if you take me to them, though. Call him."

Sarah pulled out her phone, aware of the gaping muzzle of the gun.

"What?"

Sarah wondered if that was how he answered when Cassie called.

"We have to go see her. I got the shakes. I dropped some off for you, have some for her."

"What do you think that's going to do? Check the weather, we have bigger problems."

"We need to—"

"I'm at work and have cops sitting outside. I'm sure they're listening in."

"I—" the woman jabbed at Sarah with the gun. Sarah put steel in her voice. "I don't care. She needs us. Meet me where we went last night. We have to go. Meet me at two." And she hung up.

Men don't like being talked to like that. She thought of Cassie and Derek, how she always thought they didn't treat one another with enough respect. Well, now he would have a chance to regret it, the part he'd played, anyway. Cassie, she suspected, already was. If she could feel anything.

"The weather," Sarah said. "Derek said there was a storm coming. Cassie and the girls are trapped in a culvert. If the storm hits, they're going to drown in there."

The woman grunted.

"What's your name?" Sarah said.

Unsurprisingly, the woman responded with a gruff, "You don't need to know."

"I need to call you something."

Sarah's phone buzzed, an unknown number. Derek calling back, most likely.

"I'll call you Gretta, then, until you give me something better."

Gretta grunted again and told her not to answer her phone.

"Leave your phone."

Sarah's heart twisted. Her lifeline. All her communication out into the world. A small comfort. She remembered how relieved she'd been to get back to it this morning, and there hadn't been a single new message waiting for her.

She set it on the counter. She wished Derek had never drawn her into this. She'd been trying to help her friend, goddammit. Leaving the phone, she might never hear Cassie's voice again, never see her bubbly video-making persona. Read the texts that were more real than this new reality, more Cassie.

Or maybe Gretta knew how all this worked and was just a little gruff. Maybe they all weren't well and truly fucked. Except, you know, for that woman she and Derek killed.

When Gretta indicated Sarah should leave, she did so.

The black truck smelled like leather and gun oil. Sarah didn't exactly know what gun oil smelled like, but she imagined this smell was it. Pervasive and masculine. The truck wasn't new, but it bore no personalization, nothing in the cupholders or on the floor. It wasn't pristine, but it clearly was a utilitarian vehicle. Sarah rested her head against the glass.

"How could you be so stupid?" Gretta snapped.

Sarah opened her mouth and closed it again. She always hated characters in stories who didn't share information, who made it harder for one another in unnecessary ways. A little voice in the way back of her head shouted that Gretta was going to kill her, but Marissa told her to call the number, rather adamantly, so calling the number should be a good thing, right?

Or it was a thing that would solve a problem.

"Her husband gave the shake to their daughters."

"It's not for kids. Why would he do that?" Gretta's brow furrowed. Sarah directed her, a right and a left.

"He was...mad at her? Something? So he kept the shake from her. I don't know."

"When?"

Sarah told her, indicating a secondary road they'd be on for quite some time. Without the GPS on her phone, she second-guessed herself, doubted herself. All the deserts looked the same; she hadn't been paying close enough attention. If she got them lost, would Gretta shoot her? They rode in silence, Gretta shaking her head every now and again like she was re-thinking Derek's stupidity. Sarah imagined Cassie. First her shock at seeing Arwen and Miri. Had the changes come suddenly? Then Derek—being an asshole—deliberately withholding the shakes.

It wasn't supposed to be dangerous, though. She remembered meeting Marissa, so confident and shiny. *I want to be like her.* And Sarah had been on her way. Credit cards paid off. She rented a condo, a step up from the cheap apartments she'd always lived in. She'd gotten her teeth fixed, something she was thankful for every time she smiled. Watched Cassie and Derek buy their big blocky house, four thousand square feet. "A thousand for each of us!" Cassie'd crowed. Then, with a wink, "For now."

Sarah almost asked Gretta about the baby but knew what the answer would be. Instead, she told her to take a right at the crossroads. She wished she were doing something clever, but still stupidly held on to the hope that Gretta could help. That her version of solving the problem wasn't to shoot them all, execution style.

"Will the husband come?"

Gretta's question caught her off guard.

She started to answer, "Of course!" But would he? Would he try to run? The cops knew something was up, but no idea what, of course. A mother and two children were missing, and the father was acting awful strangely. "Yes," she said.

And here they were, off the road, the culvert peeked black at them. She thought about what Derek had said about the weather. The sky wasn't so blue anymore. She reached for her phone to check Weather Underground, but it sat on the counter of the condo. The condo she was pretty sure she'd never see again.

"Wait."

Gretta paused with her hand on the door.

"Are you going to kill them?"

"You've seen them?"

Sarah opened and closed her mouth.

"What would you have me do? Give them to a zoo? To a laboratory? What is the kindest thing for your friend?"

"Fix her."

Gretta made a flat line with her mouth, except where the scar twisted up in the corner.

"Wait," Sarah said again, aware that her voice rose and sounded more frantic. "How often does this happen? What does Serenity do to people?"

The other woman sighed and opened her door. Derek's pickup truck careened into the clearing.

"It's pouring!" He leapt from the car, a shake in his hand. "Up north. It's all going to come down this way. We have to get them out." He guzzled the shake, grimacing at the vanilla flavor.

"Stop."

"Who the fuck is this?" Derek pulled the bottle from his lips, leaving himself with a '90s Got Milk? mustache.

"I called the number."

Derek looked confused, pulled the bottle away, and there was that red 1-800 number. He seemed to see Gretta, even as he drained the shake. The woman who looked ready to battle a Terminator. Or a lizard person.

"She's going to kill them," he said. He tossed the bottle into the bed of his truck.

Downlines

Gretta would kill them. The storm would kill them. Arwen was likely already dead.

"We need to save them. How do we fix this?"

"Can't save the children."

Did that mean hope for Cassie?

"One fucking shake did it, but you're telling me there's not something to reverse it? You fuckers don't have a hospital somewhere?" Gretta tried to answer. "They have mercenaries but not doctors?"

Derek went to the culvert.

"Stop," Gretta said, raising her gun, but Derek was gone. From inside, the sound of metal dragging on metal. The grate.

Sarah filtered through options. Scream? Run? Cry? Curl up in a ball?

A serpentine howl filled the air, bouncing and twisting off the corrugated metal of the culvert. A sharp cry, and Derek stumbled-ran-backed out into the sunlight, making it a few steps before falling on his ass.

Cassie leapt on him.

She was beautiful. No one could argue that. Scales covered her body, a rich copper, almost the color of her eyes. Her stomach was a lighter, yellowish color that made Sarah think of fresh cream. A nub, the beginning of a tail, jutted from her coccyx. No more sparkly manicured nails, but instead black claws, healthy and strong, reached for Derek's throat.

Sarah froze, then rushed to Derek's truck and grabbed another shake. She sprinted toward Cassie, screaming her name. "Look! Look what I have!"

Cassie's head whipped around, and Sarah saw the changes elongated her face, reducing her nose, drawing out her lips and chin into what would become a muzzle. Derek forgotten, she took the shake, swiping Sarah with a claw in the process. Blood oozed—what germs did she carry?

Gretta watched it all, as Derek got to his feet.

He looked back at the gaping maw of the culvert. "Miri? Where's Miri?"

Was Gretta so confident she could pick them all off if anyone became a real problem?

"More," Cassie's voice rasped, sounding like it hurt. "More!"

Derek dashed back into the hole as Sarah handed over another shake. There were strict instructions about how many should be consumed, though she wasn't sure those rules applied anymore. Sarah hadn't opened this one, and Cassie bit the top off, spitting it aside before she guzzled.

A crash of thunder, not too far away now, rent the afternoon. The rain would come. They would all become harder to keep track of in a downpour. Gretta would start shooting. Sarah handed over a third shake, and Cassie began to tremble.

Derek emerged from the culvert holding two limp bundles in his arms. Gretta stood by as Cassie and Sarah went to him, Sarah keeping her distance—how fast could Cassie move?

"You let them die?" His voice was a howl, filled with pain. *This is your fault*, Sarah thought. *You did this, not Cassie.* Or had Cassie done it by introducing this ridiculous product into their lives?

Cassie cried out and dropped down to her knees. Her whole body shook, and she fell to her side, convulsing. Sarah tried to go to her, but a strong hand caught her upper arm, a steel clamp.

"No. This is for them."

As her body shook on the ground, the copper of her scales diminished, turning dull. Derek hugged his children—his dead, changed children, and didn't go to his wife. Someone needed to be with Cassie! She was right, he loved the children more than he loved her. Gretta did not let Sarah go.

Blackish ichor trickled out of the corner of Cassie's mouth.

"Help her." Sarah wasn't sure if she said it out loud or not.

Finally, reluctantly, Derek went to his wife's side, set the babies down, and turned to Cassie, cradling her head. The forming muzzle seemed to have pulled back. There was Cassie's nose. She stopped shaking and opened her eyes. No more lizard slit. She panted on the dirt, chest heaving. Reached up and wiped away the blackness from the corner of her mouth. Both the black nails and the manicure were gone. Sarah wasn't sure if she even had fingernails, but supposed they would grow back.

"Is she okay?" Sarah whispered.

"No," said Gretta.

Cassie tugged at a scale, and it came off easily in her hand, pink healthy skin underneath.

"You killed them," Derek said. He thrust the tiny bodies at her.

Cassie coughed, wracking her whole body, and brought up a mass of something vile. When it was out, she sounded like herself again.

"How could you do this to us? You did this. We were never enough for you!" She lunged at him, but her weapons were all gone, the claws and teeth. "You put me in that place, you killed them."

I shouldn't be here. A ruined family sprawled before Sarah. Two dead daughters, unrecognizable in their current form. The unblemished father who started it all. Did he think he would get away with…whatever this was? And a mother who no longer had children.

Rain started to fall.

Cassie and Derek tussled on earth turning to mud beneath them.

BLAM BLAM

Thunder, no, Gretta's handgun. Sarah's ears squealed in protest, a ringing devouring all the other sounds.

Derek and Cassie, limp, falling onto one another.

Everything stopped. For a second? An hour? An eternity?

"No! She was getting better! It was over!" Sarah didn't know if she screamed or whispered the words, she couldn't hear them. Gretta hauled on a poncho and put four bodies in the bed of her truck. Even Derek she hefted with ease. A few of Cassie's scales fell off along the way, and Sarah, feeling useless, didn't even pick one up. She caught a clear glimpse of Miri, and while she wanted to remember the cheerful one-year-old, all she could see was the creature clinging to her leg and clawing at her for food. *What about Cassie's unborn baby?*

Sarah realized she could hear again when Gretta offered her a ride home.

"Never." She still wasn't sure if she was shouting or not.

"Then you'll be here, connected to his truck, connected to the body in that culvert. Maybe the flood will wash it away, maybe not. You want that?"

A part of her wanted to take some foolish moral high ground. Stay. But Gretta was right, of course. Sarah suspected Gretta was always right, and that's why she did what she did.

She stared out the window on the drive back, gripping the door handle as they passed through standing water deeper than should be driven through. But they prevailed. She could go to the police once she was home. Could be the whistleblower the world had been waiting for. Expose Serenity, founder Mark Morris…he must know about the side effects of his product if he had a goon squad on speed dial. Goon squad on speed dial. Sarah suspected she knew what would happen to a whistleblower. Thought long and hard about the "in memoriam" section of the annual conference. She realized she was staring at Gretta's gun when Gretta said, "You will forget."

Not a question. Sarah nodded like an idiot. If she didn't forget, she would be dead just like Cassie and her family.

If Gretta had let them live, they'd both have gone to jail. Two daughters were dead. Missing, they'd have to be. Couldn't produce bodies of…lizard people. What would happen to them in jail when they couldn't have their Serenity?

And Sarah? She'd killed a woman. Not with her own hands, but close enough. Should she ask Gretta to end her as well? She thought of her empty condo. Her downlines. It wasn't much worth living for. She didn't even have a job anymore; she'd never touch Serenity or the company again.

Gretta pulled up outside the condo, rain pouring down in sheets. She said nothing. Sarah wanted to ask, but bit it all back. She didn't want to know. Sarah would disappear. Maybe back to the East Coast. Maybe make a profit on the condo. Maybe get a fish. Something more than a house plant. A lizard. Something to take care of, something to love. She would find her own joy, just not her own serenity.

About the Author

Ghosties and ghoulies and long-leggedy beasties and things that go bump in the night: That's Kirstin Dearborn in a nutshell. This life-long New Englander and horror writer was destined to write about anything that screams, squelches, or bleeds. Her first literary love was Michael Crichton (she was eleven). Her second, Stephen King. And *Jurassic Park,* one of her favorite movies, she asserts is a creature feature—her favorite type of horror flick.

At the University of Maine, Dearborn studied theater and English, and then went on to Seton Hill University where she earned her M.F.A. in Writing Popular Fiction (heavy on the monster horror). She's been on the horror scene since 2010 with her short stories and novellas, and has contributed to a number of anthologies.

Dearborn is the author of *The Amazing Alligator Girl* (2022), *Sacrifice Island* (2018), *Woman in White* (2017), *Whispers* (2016), *Stolen Away* (2016), and *Trinity* (2012).

If Dearborn is taking a break from all things blood-curdling, she's likely scaling high peaks, zipping around Vermont on a motorcycle, hanging out with her pets, or gallivanting the globe looking for her next novel's horrifying inspiration.

Curious about other Crossroad Press books? Stop by our
website: http://crossroadpress.com
We offer quality writing
in digital, audio, and print formats.

Subscribe to our newsletter on the website homepage and
receive a free eBook.